Happy Birthday!

Ellie Slater
1-27-09

This book has been placed in the Peach Plains Elementary
School Library in honor of this person's birthday.

FRIENDSHIP STORIES
You Can Share

SeaStar Books

NEW YORK

Special thanks to Amy Cohn, Leigh Ann Jones, Valerie Lewis, and Walter Mayes for the consultation services and invaluable support they provided for the creation of this book.

Reading Rainbow® is a production of GPN/Nebraska ETV and WNED-TV Buffalo and is produced by Lancit Media Entertainment, Ltd., a JuniorNet Company. *Reading Rainbow®* is a registered trademark of GPN/WNED-TV.

The following are gratefully acknowledged for granting permission to reprint the material in this book: "Alone" from *Days With Frog and Toad.* Copyright © 1979 by Arnold Lobel. Used by permission of HarperCollins Publishers. • Excerpt from "Mr. Putter and Tabby" from *Mr. Putter and Tabby Pour the Tea.* Text copyright © 1994 by Cynthia Rylant. Illustrations copyright © 1994 by Arthur Howard. Reprinted by permission of Harcourt, Inc. • Text and selected illustrations from *The Hating Book.* Text copyright © 1969 by Charlotte Zolotow. Illustrations copyright © 1969 by Ben Shecter. Used by permission of HarperCollins Publishers. • "The Book" from *George and Martha Back in Town* by James Marshall. Copyright © 1984 by James Marshall. Used by permission of Houghton Mifflin Company. All rights reserved. • "A Summer Day" from *Jake and the Copycats* by Joanne Rocklin and Janet Pedersen. Text copyright © 1998 by Joanne Rocklin. Illustrations copyright © 1998 by Janet Pedersen. Used by permission of Random House Children's Books, a division of Random House, Inc.

 SeaStar Books • A division of North-South Books Inc.

ISBN 1-58717-083-3 (reinforced trade binding) 10 9 8 7 6 5 4 3 2 1
ISBN 1-58717-084-1 (paperback edition) 10 9 8 7 6 5 4 3 2 1

Contents

Alone

BY Arnold Lobel

Toad went to Frog's house.

He found a note on the door.

The note said,

"Dear Toad,

I am not at home.

I went out.

I want to be alone."

"Alone?" said Toad.

"Frog has me for a friend.

Why does he want to be alone?"

Toad looked through the windows.

He looked in the garden.

He did not see Frog.

Toad went to the woods.

Frog was not there.

He went to the meadow.

Frog was not there.

Toad went down to the river.

There was Frog.

He was sitting on an island
by himself.

"Poor Frog," said Toad.
"He must be very sad.
I will cheer him up."
Toad ran home.
He made sandwiches.
He made a pitcher of iced tea.

He put everything
in a basket.

Toad hurried
back to the river.
"Frog," he shouted,
"it's me.
It's your best friend, Toad!"
Frog was too far away to hear.
Toad took off his jacket
and waved it like a flag.
Frog was too far away to see.
Toad shouted and waved,
but it was no use.

Frog sat on the island.

He did not see or hear Toad.

A turtle swam by.

Toad climbed on the turtle's back.

"Turtle," said Toad,

"carry me to the island.

Frog is there.

He wants to be alone."

"If Frog wants to be alone,"
said the turtle,
"why don't you leave him alone?"
"Maybe you are right," said Toad.
"Maybe Frog does not
want to see me.
Maybe he does not want me
to be his friend anymore."
"Yes, maybe," said the turtle
as he swam to the island.

"Frog!" cried Toad.
"I am sorry for all
the dumb things I do.
I am sorry for all
the silly things I say.
Please be my friend!"
Toad slipped off the turtle.
With a splash, he fell in the river.

Frog pulled Toad
up onto the island.
Toad looked in the basket.
The sandwiches were wet.
The pitcher of iced tea was empty.
"Our lunch is spoiled," said Toad.
"I made it for you, Frog,
so that you would be happy."

"But Toad," said Frog.
"I am happy. I am very happy.
This morning
when I woke up
I felt good because
the sun was shining.
I felt good because
I was a frog.
And I felt good because
I have you for a friend.
I wanted to be alone.
I wanted to think about
how fine everything is."

"Oh," said Toad.
"I guess that is a good reason
for wanting to be alone."
"Now," said Frog,
"I will be glad *not* to be alone.
Let's eat lunch."

Frog and Toad
stayed on the island
all afternoon.
They ate wet sandwiches
without iced tea.
They were two close friends
sitting alone together.

Mr. Putter and Tabby

BY Cynthia Rylant

PICTURES BY Arthur Howard

In the mornings
Mr. Putter and Tabby liked to share
an English muffin.
Mr. Putter ate his with jam.
Tabby ate hers with cream cheese.

In the afternoons
Mr. Putter and Tabby
liked to share tea.
Mr. Putter took his with sugar.
Tabby took hers with cream.

And in the evenings
they sat by the window,
and Mr. Putter told stories.
He told the most wonderful stories.
Each story made Tabby purr.

On summer days they warmed their
old bones together in the sun.
On fall days they took
long walks through the trees.
And on winter days they turned
the opera up *very* loud.

After a while it seemed as if
they had always lived together.
Tabby knew just what Mr. Putter
was going to do next.
Mr. Putter knew just where Tabby
was going to sleep next.

In the mornings each looked for the other as soon as they opened their eyes.

And at night each looked for
the other as their eyes were closing.
Mr. Putter could not remember
life without Tabby.

Tabby could not remember
life without Mr. Putter.
They lived among their
tulips and trees.

They ate their muffins.

They poured their tea.

They turned up the opera,

and enjoyed the most
perfect company of all—

each other.

SELECTIONS FROM

The Hating Book

BY Charlotte Zolotow

PICTURES BY Ben Shecter

I hate hate hated
my friend.

When I moved over in the school bus,
she sat somewhere else.
When her point broke in arithmetic
and I passed her my pencil,
she took Peter's instead.

"Ask her," my mother said,
"ask your friend why."
But I wouldn't,
I couldn't,
I'd rather die.

What if she should say
Oh, please, just go away.
You're ugly and dumb.
Being with you
was never fun.
Oh, I hated my friend.

When it was her turn
to wash the board,
she didn't ask me to help.

When it was time to choose teams,
she didn't choose me.
And when I made a basket
and everyone else yelled Y A A A A,
she turned away.

When I went to walk home with her,
she had already gone.
When she took her dog out
and I whistled to him,
she put him on a leash
and led him away.

Oh, I hated my friend.

"Ask her," my mother said,
"ask her why."

I couldn't,
I'd rather die.

No—

if that's the way she's going to be,

it's quite okay with me.

"Ask her," my mother said,

"ask and see…"

I wouldn't,

I couldn't.

But maybe…

"You've been so rotten," I said.
"Why?"
She looked as though she'd cry.
"It's you," she said. "Last week
when I wore my new dress,
Sue said Jane said you said
I looked like a freak."
"I did not!
I said you looked *neat*!"

She looked straight at me for a while,
and then we both began to smile.
My friend said, "Hey,
maybe tomorrow we can play?"
"Oh, yes," I said, "OKAY!"

I didn't hate her anyway.
I wish it were tomorrow.

The Book

BY James Marshall

George was all nice and cozy.

"May I join you?" said Martha.

"I'm reading," said George.

"I'll be as quiet as a mouse,"
said Martha.

"Thank you," said George.

And he went back to his book.

But soon Martha was fidgeting.

"Please!" said George.

"Have some consideration!"

"Sorry," said Martha.

George went back to his reading.

But in no time
Martha was fidgeting again.

"That does it!" said George.

And he left.

At home he got
all nice and cozy again.

He opened his book.

"It is important to be
considerate to our friends,"
said the book.

"It certainly *is*!" said George.

"Sometimes we are thoughtless
without even knowing it,"
said the book.
"*I'll* say!" said George.
"Martha should read this book."

He went to find her.

"I'm sorry I was fidgeting,"
said Martha. "I got lonely."

"Oh," said George.
"I never considered that."

"What did you want to tell me?"
said Martha.

"Oh nothing," said George.
"I just got lonely too."

And they sat and told stories
into the night.

Martha didn't fidget even once.

A Summer Day

BY Joanne Rocklin

PICTURES BY Janet Pedersen

"Nothing to do around here.
Bo-ring," said Jake Biddle.
"Bo-ring," said his brother, Pete.
"Go outside and play,"
said Mrs. Biddle.
"Who can I play with?" asked Jake.
"My best friend, Max, is away!"
"Play with your brother,"
said Mrs. Biddle.
"He's a baby," said Jake.
Jake did a somersault off the couch.
Pete did a somersault off the couch.
"He's a copycat, too," said Jake.

Outside, Jake flopped down
under the lemon tree.
Pete flopped down beside him.
"Move over," said Jake. "You stink."
"*You* stink," said Pete.
"You double stink," said Jake.
"*You* double stink," said Pete.
"Triple stink," said Jake.
"Triple stink," said Pete.
Jake did not know what came next.
"Copycat," he said.

Just then Jake's cat, Fanny, walked by.
"My cat is the smartest cat
on the planet Earth!" said Jake.
"Not on the whole *planet*!" said Pete.
"In the whole universe," said Jake.
"On Mercury, Venus, Mars, Jupiter,
Saturn, Uranus, and Pluto, too."
Jake had learned lots of things
in first grade.

There is one more planet,
thought Jake.
He could not remember it.
But Pete would not know
there was one more planet.
Pete had not learned about planets
in kindergarten.

"Fanny can do tricks," said Jake.
Jake snapped his fingers.
"Roll over, Fanny!" said Jake.
Fanny rolled onto her back.
"She just wants her
tummy scratched," said Pete.

"Stay, Fanny," said Jake.

Fanny stayed.

"Ha! Some trick," said Pete.

He tossed a twig near Fanny.

"Fetch, Fanny!" Pete called.

Fanny yawned at the twig.

"Cats don't fetch," said Jake.

"Everybody knows that."

"Ha! The smartest cat
in the universe would fetch,"
said Pete.

"You stink," said Jake.

"*You* stink," said Pete.

Jake and Pete chased each other
around the lemon tree.
They had a somersault race.

They sprayed each other
with the garden hose.

Then they flopped down
beside Fanny.
Mrs. Biddle came outside.
She had ice cream bars
and lemonade.
"Having fun?"
Mrs. Biddle asked.
"Sort of," said Jake.
"Sort of," said Pete.